Little, Brown and Company

Hachette Book Group
237 Park Avenue, New York, NY 10017
Visit our website at www.lb-kids.com

Little, Brown and Company is a division of Hachette Book Group, Inc.
The Little, Brown name and logo are trademarks of Hachette Book Group, Inc.

The publisher is not responsible for websites (or their content) that are not owned by the publisher.

First Edition: April 2013

ISBN 978-0-316-22814-5

Library of Congress Control Number: 2012946972

10 9 8 7 6 5 4 3 2 1

LEO

Printed in China

Welcome TO Equestria!

By Olivia London

LITTLE, BROWN AND COMPANY
New York   Boston

"Hey, Spike!" Twilight Sparkle calls out as her favorite baby dragon and number-one assistant runs into the library.

"Hey, Twilight," he replies. "You got a letter from Shining Armor and Princess Cadance!"

"Well, what does it say?" Twilight asks excitedly.

Dear Twilight Sparkle,

As the new rulers of the Crystal Empire, we have received many warm invitations to visit towns throughout Equestria, including Ponyville! We are delighted to come visit you and your friends, and we look forward to seeing your new home. Until then, we promise to send postcards from our journey. See you soon!

Love always,
Shining Armor
& Princess Cadance

"Did you hear that, Spike?" Twilight cries out. "My brother and Princess Cadance are coming! I can't wait to tell everypony!"

From a tall tower in the Crystal Castle, Shining Armor and Princess Cadance see clear across their glittering kingdom.

"I will miss our home while we are away," Princess Cadance says, "but I am excited for our trip!"

"Me, too," Shining Armor replies. "We'd better get going!"

"That's true. Oh, I don't want to forget this gift for Twilight!" the princess says, slipping a package into her satchel.

The couple spend the rest of the morning saying farewell to all the Crystal Ponies in their kingdom.

Finally, it is time for them to board their flying carriage and take off!

After a short while, the newlyweds arrive at their first destination: Canterlot! The majestic city where they grew up was also the setting for their beautiful wedding. They are delighted to visit Princess Celestia and Princess Luna at Canterlot Castle, and enjoy some time in the city together.

Dear Twilight,

We arrived in Canterlot today after a lovely send-off in the Crystal Empire. It was wonderful to enjoy Canterlot knowing that it is now safe from that evil Queen Chrysalis! We went to the derby to watch the races, and we spent the night with Princess Luna. She took us to the observatory in your old library, where we watched her raise the moon. Then we went into town to see some shops. Cadance remembered how much your friend Rarity loves fashion, so she picked up a little something special for her. Our next stop is Cloudsdale! We'll write again soon.

Much love,

Shining Armor (& Princess Cadance)

"Look! The Wonderbolts are performing a brand-new routine to welcome us," Shining Armor points out as they touch down in Cloudsdale. "They must have practiced for weeks."

Cadance says, "While we are here, we must visit the hardworking Pegasi, who make all of Equestria's weather in the weather factory. Let's remember to thank them for bringing sunshine to the Crystal Faire every year."

"I think this will be a short visit," Shining Armor murmurs to himself as he wonders how to get from cloud to cloud without wings. "Now I remember why this city is home to only Pegasus ponies!" He laughs.

Dear Twilight Sparkle,

Today we arrived in Cloudsdale just in time to judge the Best Young Flyer competition. Being here reminds us of the time when your friend Rainbow Dash won the grand prize by performing a Sonic Rainboom. It must have been thrilling! I found something that made me think of her and will bring it with us to Ponyville. Looking forward to seeing you soon!

Always,

Princess Cadance (& your loving brother)

"Our next stop is Appleloosa," Shining Armor tells Cadance, looking down at the map.

"Yes, Applejack told me all about Appleloosa at our wedding," Cadance remembers. "It is a small town best known for its delicious apple orchards. And it took the ponies there only one year to build it!"

"That's impressive," says Shining Armor. "Doesn't Applejack's cousin Braeburn live here?" Cadance nods.

When the couple arrive, the town of Appleloosa is decorated in their honor, and Braeburn shows them around.

APPLELOOSA

Dearest Twilight,

The orchards of Appleloosa are in full bloom, and Braeburn has been an incredibly gracious host. He says to tell you that the ponies and buffalo are still getting along well. We saw the tree that Applejack planted when you and your friends came to visit, and we are bringing her a little something special from one apple orchard to another! It's time for us to get going now. More later...

Your loving brother,
Shining Armor

"We have a very busy schedule in Manehattan," Princess Cadance tells her beloved as they fly over the city skyline toward their next stop. "We've been invited to a gala every night! This really is the most cosmopolitan city in all of Equestria. The *Manehattaner* will have reporters following us everywhere."

Shining Armor isn't as interested in the parties. "Let's ride the underground pony express train—it's called the Maneway," he says.

MANEHATTAN

Dear Twilight,

Manehattan is a very impressive city. The buildings are as tall as the sky, and the society is very sophisticated. But all the ponies here rush around like they're in a hurry! It's a bit fast-paced for us.

We tried some of the most delicious pastries we have ever tasted and knew at once that we must bring a treat for Pinkie Pie, who is so fond of sweets. We are now only a few short stops away from Ponyville!

Love,
Princess Cadance

The next few days are a whirlwind of adventure. They visit the town of Dodge Junction, the city of Fillydelphia, and Las Pegasus. In each town, the newlyweds and new leaders of the Crystal Empire are welcomed with open arms and a lovely party.

At last, it is time to go to Ponyville. But flying over a forest, they start to tire. Cadance decides they need to rest, so they land right next to a small hut, where a zebra named Zecora lives.

Zecora tells them all about the secrets of the forest and points out several interesting creatures to be careful of, such as timber wolves, sea serpents, and parasprites, all of which call the Everfree Forest home.

Dear Twilight,

Today we made a surprise stop in the Everfree Forest and had the most interesting day. Did you know that the forest doesn't work like the rest of the land? The plants and animals in the forest all fend for themselves. Clouds here can even move without the Pegasus ponies' help! We met someone who asked us to bring a special package to Fluttershy.

Anyway, we enjoyed our detour very much, but we will arrive in Ponyville tomorrow!

Love,
Shining Armor

EVERFREE FOREST

The next day, Twilight and the mayor of Ponyville are already waiting for them in the town square.

"Welcome, Your Majesties," says the mayor.

"I'm so happy you're here!" Twilight cries out to them.

"Hi, Twilight," Shining Armor says, giving his little sister a hug.

"It's so good to see you," Cadance says with a swish of her tail.

"Are you ready to tour Ponyville?" Twilight asks, already leading the way. "This is the town square, and Ponyville Park, and the Day Spa. And there's the marketplace, where many ponies sell their goods. And this is Golden Oak Library— it's where Spike and I live. Come inside!"

"Would you like to see where all my friends live?" Twilight asks them.

"We would love to," Cadance replies, "and we can give them the gifts we picked up for them on our journey. But before we go, this is for you, Twilight. It's something from our home, so that you will always have a piece of us with you."

"Thank you!" Twilight shouts with glee. She unwraps a photograph of her brother and new sister-in-law in a hoofmade frame. "I love it!"

They set out to see the other ponies. "This is where Rainbow Dash lives. She controls our weather with the help of her fellow Pegasi," Twilight explains at the first house, which they have to get a lift to.

Shining Armor gives Rainbow Dash her gift: a pair of official Wonderbolts flying goggles.

"Thanks. This is awesome!" Rainbow Dash yells, putting on the goggles.

"This is SugarCube Corner, where Pinkie Pie lives. Downstairs is the bakery, where she works," Twilight says next.

"And this is the most decadent cupcake you'll ever taste," Princess Cadance says to Pinkie. "We had one in Manehattan and thought of you."

"Oh, thank you! I can't wait to eat it!" Pinkie Pie replies, jumping up and down. She sneaks a lick of the frosting. "Mmmmm!"

"This is Rarity's dress shop, the Carousel Boutique!" Twilight says, stopping in the store.

"Hello," Rarity greets them. "What an honor to have you in my shop."

"I thought you could make some use out of these fine new silks that just arrived at the fabric shop in Canterlot when we were there," the princess says, handing them to Rarity.

"Oh, thank you, Princess! I'm going to design some fabulous new couture with these!" Rarity coos. "Maybe you will wear one to a royal ball someday!"

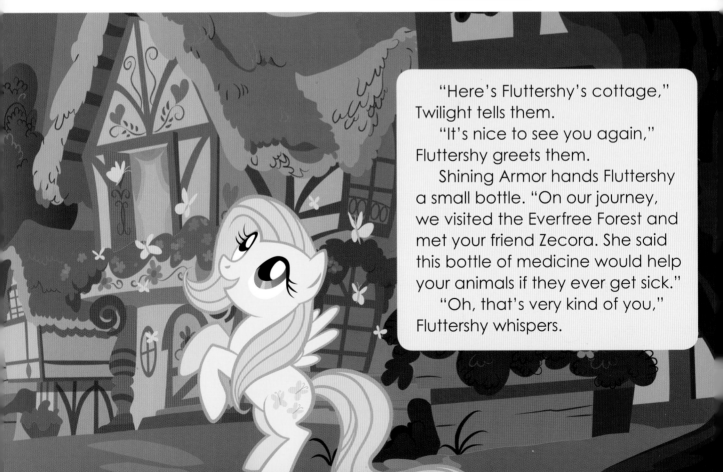

"Here's Fluttershy's cottage," Twilight tells them.

"It's nice to see you again," Fluttershy greets them.

Shining Armor hands Fluttershy a small bottle. "On our journey, we visited the Everfree Forest and met your friend Zecora. She said this bottle of medicine would help your animals if they ever get sick."

"Oh, that's very kind of you," Fluttershy whispers.

"And this is Sweet Apple Acres. It's owned by Applejack and her family," Twilight says, leading Cadance and Shining Armor through the gate of a pretty farm.

"Welcome to Sweet Apple Acres!" Applejack calls out as she gallops up to them.

"Thank you," Shining Armor replies. "Your cousin was a wonderful tour guide in Appleloosa. We brought you a little something from an old friend: an apple from your tree, Bloomberg."

"Well, that's mighty nice of you both!" Applejack cheers.

"What a pretty town, Twilight," Cadance remarks. "No wonder you love it here."

"Ponyville is great," Twilight agrees. "But the reason I love it so much is because this is where I have so many friends. After all, isn't that what really makes a home?"

"You are much wiser than when you were a little foal," Cadance replies. "I am so proud of you." She gives Twilight a big hug.

Dearest Twilight,

We are finally home in the Crystal Empire, and while we are happy to be back, we miss traveling already! We had a wonderful time in Ponyville with you and your friends. Perhaps the next time we travel across Equestria, you could come with us. Until then, we look forward to having you and your friends as our guests here in the Crystal Empire, so please come visit us soon!

With love,
Princess Cadance & Shining Armor